Mary's Story

For Eamonn, Elyssia, Daniel, Karen and Peter — S. J. B.
For Grandma Bowgen, with love — H. C.

Barefoot Books
37 West 17th Street
Fourth Floor East
New York, New York 10010

This book is printed on 100% acid-free paper. Typeset in Bembo 15 point on 22 point leading
The illustrations were prepared in watercolor, graphite and collage on 140lb. Bockingford paper
Graphic design by Judy Linard, London. Color separation by Grafiscan, Italy
Printed and bound in Singapore by Tien Wah Press (Pte) Ltd
1 3 5 7 9 8 6 4 2
Publisher Cataloging-in-Publication Data
Boss, Sarah.
    Mary's story / written by Sarah Jane Boss ; illustrated
by Helen Cann.—1st ed.
[40]p. : col. ill. ;   cm.
Summary: Traces the life of the Virgin Mary from her
childhood to her assumption. Well-known Bible stories
are viewed through her eyes, offering a new and
refreshing perspective. Beautifully illustrated throughout
by artwork inspired by the paintings of the Italian
Renaissance..
ISBN 1-901223-44-2
1. Mary, Blessed Virgin, Saint — Biography — Juvenile literature.
2. Bible stories—N.T.—Juvenile literature. I. Cann, Helen, ill. II. Title.
232.91 [B]—dc21   1999   AC   CIP

Mary's Story

Written by Sarah Jane Boss
Illustrated by Helen Cann

BAREFOOT BOOKS

Long ago, in the city of Jerusalem, there stood a temple which was the house of the Lord God. In a nearby town there lived a woman named Anne, who was married to a man named Joachim. Anne and Joachim were kind people. They loved God and they helped their neighbors, but as the years went by they became very sad because they did not have any children, and this was what they wanted more than anything else.

One day when she was in her garden, Anne felt so sad that she started to cry. She prayed to God, saying, "Lord, even the birds in the trees have their little ones, but I do not. Please let me have a child."

As she sat weeping, an extraordinary thing happened. An angel from God appeared before her, and the angel said, "Anne, Anne! God has heard your prayer, and you will have a child who will be famous throughout the world."

Another angel took the same message to Joachim, as he was looking after his sheep in the fields. Anne and Joachim were so thrilled that they each ran to find the other. They met at the Golden Gate of the temple in Jerusalem. They flung their arms around each other and hugged each other for joy. Then they went home together.

Anne gave birth to a baby girl, just as the angel had said. And they called the baby Mary.

Because Mary was born as the answer to a prayer, her parents wanted her whole life to be offered to God. When she was three years old, they took her to the temple in Jerusalem. Right away, Mary loved being there. She danced on the temple steps as she went up to meet the priest, and everyone who saw her loved her.

As Mary grew up, her mother taught her to read. Mary also liked to visit the temple. She spent hours listening to the priests as they chanted psalms, and watching the people coming and going, but she also liked to sit quietly with her eyes closed and say her own prayers.

When Mary was sixteen years old, she was engaged to be married to a man named Joseph. They lived in the village of Nazareth. Before their wedding day, however, a wonderful thing happened – something so wonderful that people have remembered Mary ever since. One day, while Mary was drawing water from the village well, the angel Gabriel appeared before her and said, "Rejoice, Mary, you are most favored, the Lord is with you!"

Mary was bewildered by this, but then the angel spoke again: "Do not be afraid, Mary, for God has looked on you with favor. You are going to have a son, and you will call him

Jesus. He will be great, and will rule over a kingdom that will last forever."

But Mary asked, "How can this be, since I am a virgin?"

"The Holy Spirit will come upon you," said the angel, "and your child shall be called the Son of God. And know this, too. Your cousin Elizabeth is also to have a son, even though she is old and people thought that she could never have children. For with God, nothing is impossible."

Then Mary said, "Behold, I am the handmaid of the Lord. Let what you have said be done to me according to His word." And the angel left her.

Afterward, Mary felt very excited by the angel's news, and she set off right away to visit Elizabeth. The two cousins laughed and sang together and Mary stayed with Elizabeth for many weeks. When Elizabeth's son was born, she and her husband named him John. After his birth, Mary returned to her home.

Meanwhile, Joseph had a dream in which an angel told him about the baby that Mary was to have. The angel said, "Mary's child is of the Holy Spirit. You must call him Jesus. This name means 'the Lord saves,' because Jesus will save his people from evil." So Joseph knew that he would have to take very good care of Mary's son.

When it was nearly time for Mary to give birth to her baby, she and Joseph had to go on a journey to Bethlehem. Mary rode on the back of their donkey, and Joseph led the way.

The journey was slow and uncomfortable. They traveled for several days and by the time they reached Bethlehem, the town was very full. Mary and Joseph went from one inn to the next, but they could not find a room anywhere. At last, a kind innkeeper offered the young couple shelter in a cave

where he kept his animals. Joseph used straw and clothes to make a bed for Mary, and Jesus was born that very night. She did not have a crib, so Mary laid him in the manger, on the sweet-smelling hay. The animals did not mind having a baby on the hay that was their food because they knew that this child was from God. The ox rubbed its nose against little Jesus to keep him warm. Mary was so happy that she did not mind how cold and uncomfortable it was in the cave.

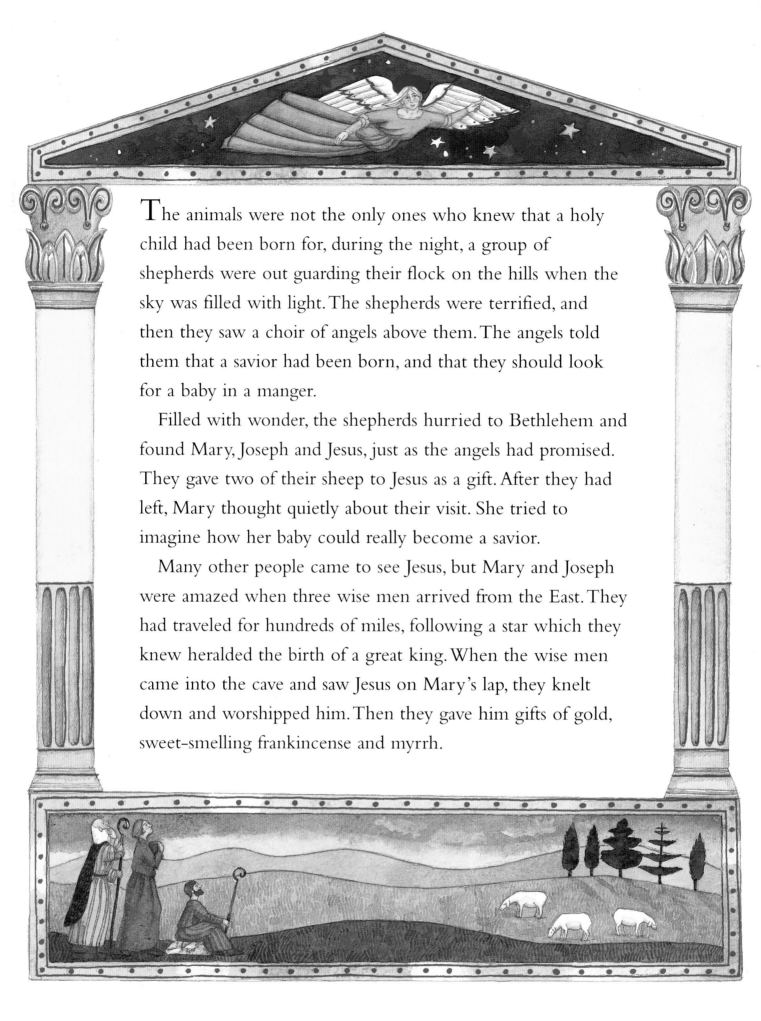

The animals were not the only ones who knew that a holy child had been born for, during the night, a group of shepherds were out guarding their flock on the hills when the sky was filled with light. The shepherds were terrified, and then they saw a choir of angels above them. The angels told them that a savior had been born, and that they should look for a baby in a manger.

Filled with wonder, the shepherds hurried to Bethlehem and found Mary, Joseph and Jesus, just as the angels had promised. They gave two of their sheep to Jesus as a gift. After they had left, Mary thought quietly about their visit. She tried to imagine how her baby could really become a savior.

Many other people came to see Jesus, but Mary and Joseph were amazed when three wise men arrived from the East. They had traveled for hundreds of miles, following a star which they knew heralded the birth of a great king. When the wise men came into the cave and saw Jesus on Mary's lap, they knelt down and worshipped him. Then they gave him gifts of gold, sweet-smelling frankincense and myrrh.

Forty days after Jesus was born, Mary went to the temple to be blessed. Joseph went with her, and they took Jesus, too, to present him to the Lord. In the temple they met two holy people, an old man named Simeon and an old woman named Anna. Both of them were overjoyed when they saw Jesus, and the old man took Jesus in his arms and prayed, "Lord, now let Your servant depart in peace, for my eyes have seen the salvation of the world, a light to enlighten the Gentiles, and the glory of Your people Israel."

Then he turned to Mary and said, "A sword of sorrow will pierce through your own soul."

Indeed, Mary was to suffer very much because of her son.

Not long after this, an angel spoke to Joseph in a dream. The angel said, "King Herod wants to kill Jesus, so you must escape from him. Take Mary and Jesus to Egypt and stay there."

King Herod had heard that a king had been born in Bethlehem, and he did not want another king. So he sent soldiers to murder all the little boys under two years old, but Mary and Joseph were already on their way to Egypt, so Jesus

was safe. Yet Mary often felt sad and frightened in this strange country. She heard about the baby boys who had been killed, and although she was glad that her baby was safe, she was also full of sorrow at the death of so many innocent children.

Then one night, the angel appeared to Joseph again, saying, "It is safe for you to go home." So Mary, Joseph and Jesus returned quietly to Nazareth.

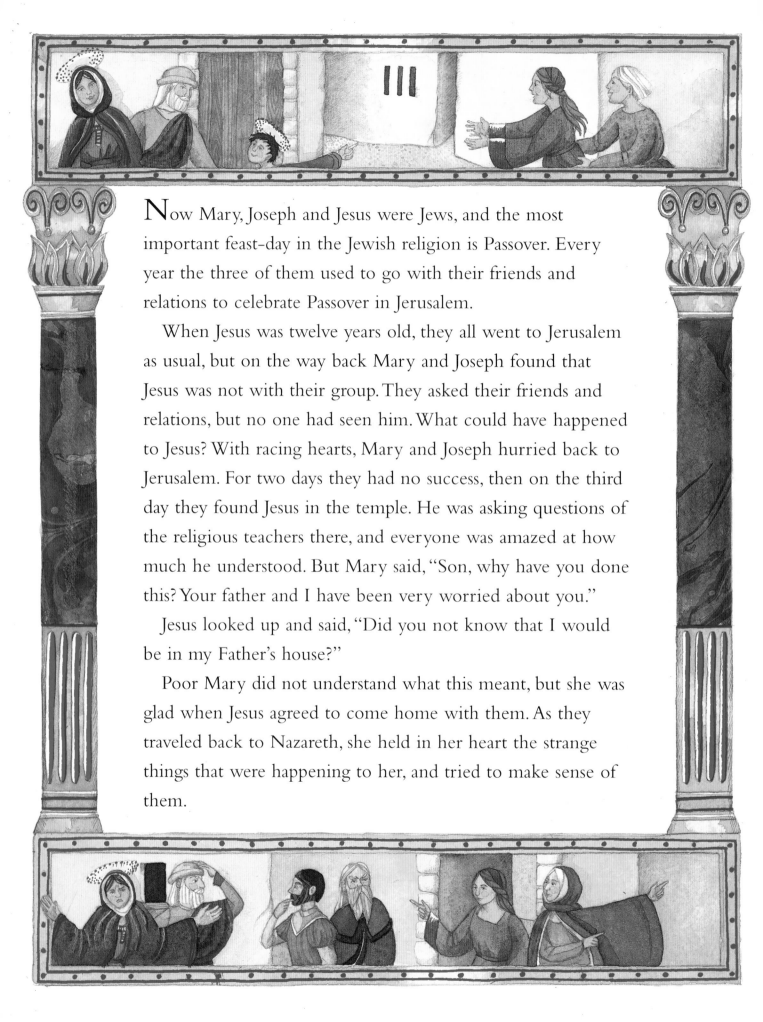

Now Mary, Joseph and Jesus were Jews, and the most important feast-day in the Jewish religion is Passover. Every year the three of them used to go with their friends and relations to celebrate Passover in Jerusalem.

When Jesus was twelve years old, they all went to Jerusalem as usual, but on the way back Mary and Joseph found that Jesus was not with their group. They asked their friends and relations, but no one had seen him. What could have happened to Jesus? With racing hearts, Mary and Joseph hurried back to Jerusalem. For two days they had no success, then on the third day they found Jesus in the temple. He was asking questions of the religious teachers there, and everyone was amazed at how much he understood. But Mary said, "Son, why have you done this? Your father and I have been very worried about you."

Jesus looked up and said, "Did you not know that I would be in my Father's house?"

Poor Mary did not understand what this meant, but she was glad when Jesus agreed to come home with them. As they traveled back to Nazareth, she held in her heart the strange things that were happening to her, and tried to make sense of them.

Now, Joseph was a carpenter and he taught Jesus to be a carpenter, too. Mary was pleased that her husband and son were craftsmen, and while they worked she used to spin thread and have it woven into cloth to make clothes for them all.

While Jesus grew up, he lived and worked with his parents.

Then Joseph died. He and Mary had always helped each other and loved each other very much, so after her husband's death Mary wept and could not eat her food because she was so sad. But Jesus looked after her and comforted her, and in time she started to feel better.

Mary and Jesus both liked going to parties, and one day they were invited to a wedding in a town called Cana. There were many guests at the wedding, and there was plenty of food for them to eat, but halfway through the wedding the wine ran out. Mary went to Jesus and said, "Look! They have no more wine!" Then she turned to the servants and said, "Do whatever he tells you."

Jesus told the servants to fill six stone jars with water. They did this, and when they poured the water out again, what the guests tasted was not water, but wine. It was the best wine they had ever drunk.

After this, Jesus started to go around the countryside, talking to anyone who would listen, and healing people who were ill. He told the people who came to him, "Do not worry about anything. Trust your Father in Heaven, because He cares for everything that He has made."

Jesus also said, "Be sorry for the things you have done wrong, and care for those who are poor or sick."

As he taught, more and more people followed Jesus. After a while, he called together a group of twelve men to help him. They are often called the apostles. There were also women who traveled with him and gave him food and clothing.

Mary did not know where Jesus went as he taught, but she heard stories about his miracles from people passing through Nazareth, and she wondered what would happen to him.

One day, Mary heard some very bad news. Jesus's cousin
John, Elizabeth's son, had been killed by King Herod. John was
a holy man, and Mary thought, "If John is dead, perhaps Jesus
also will be in danger."

Soon after this, more and more people started to say that
Jesus would be put to death. The rulers of the country
argued, "This man is teaching people that God is the only

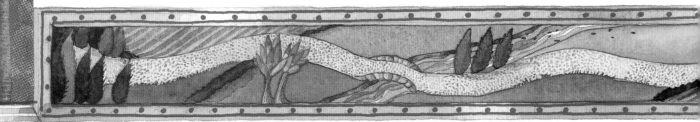

king. The people will not obey us if they think that God's laws are the only ones which matter." So the rulers wanted to get Jesus out of the way.

Then, just before Passover, a friend of Mary's came rushing to her house and said, "Mary! Mary! I think they are going to kill him!" So Mary put on her cloak and traveled as fast as she could to Jerusalem.

It was Friday. When Mary arrived, she found a great crowd of men and women pushing their way through the streets. At the head of the crowd there were soldiers. Then Mary saw that behind the soldiers there was a man carrying a huge wooden cross on his back, and next to him was Jesus. Mary cried, "I must get to my son!" And she pushed her way through the milling crowd.

Poor Jesus! He had a crown of sharp thorns on his head and his body was bruised and bleeding. Mary threw her arms round him and kissed him. And then she said, "Remember I love you." And Jesus stopped and said to her, "God will make it all right in the end."

Mary went with the soldiers and the other people and they climbed up a hill. A little bird, a goldfinch, flew down to Jesus. It wanted to take away his pain, so it pulled out one of the thorns from his head. Mary smiled through her tears as the goldfinch flew off. Then the soldiers laid Jesus on the cross and nailed him to it through his hands and feet. After this, they raised the cross so that it stood upright on the top of the hill.

Mary stood by the cross beside a young man called John. John was one of the twelve apostles, and Jesus loved him very much.

As Jesus hung on the cross, he said to Mary, "Woman, this is your son." And to John he said, "This is your mother." From that day on, John made a place for Mary in his home.

Then the sky grew dark and although it was still daytime, the sun disappeared. In Jerusalem, the curtain of the temple was torn in two. Jesus cried out with a loud voice, "Father, into Your hands I commend my spirit!" Then he died.

Jesus's friends buried him in a tomb. They loved him more than anyone else in the world, and they all wept and cried out, "What shall we do without Jesus?" And no one wept more than Mary.

All the next day, Mary sat thinking about her son. On the third day, which was Sunday, she was still wondering at all the things that had happened when there was a knock on the door and a group of women hurried in.

"Mary!" they cried. "Jesus is alive! He is risen from the dead! His tomb is empty! We have seen him and he has spoken to us!"

After this, Jesus's followers saw him again several times and talked with him. He told them, "God will send you the Holy Spirit. You must carry on teaching as I have done."

Then, after forty days, he was taken up to Heaven and they did not see him again.

Mary stayed in Jerusalem with the followers of Jesus and they prayed together every day. One morning, while they were at prayer, they heard a sound like rushing wind. Then tongues which seemed to be of fire came to rest upon their heads. The Holy Spirit came upon them, and no matter what country they came from it seemed to the people listening that they were hearing their own language. Jesus's followers laughed with joy and shouted, "Now the whole world will know about Jesus!"

This group of men and women were the first Christians, and Mary was one of them.

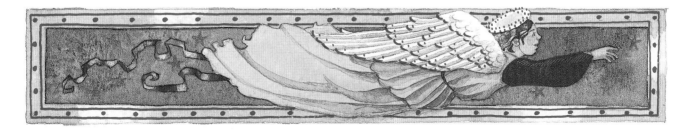

When Mary grew old, the angel Gabriel came to her once more. He was holding a branch from a palm tree, and he said, "I greet you as the mother of Jesus Christ our Lord. Soon you will be with your son again."

Mary lay down on her bed and closed her eyes. The apostles came to her bedside with the women who were her dear friends. And so her life on earth came to an end. The apostles buried Mary in a tomb in a garden in Jerusalem. On the third day, they went back to the place where Mary was buried. But when they arrived, the tomb was empty, and they saw Mary being taken up to Heaven. They smiled with delight and said, "Now Mary will be with Jesus in Heaven forevermore."

Author's Note

The principal stories about Mary's life are contained in the Gospels. Luke Chapters 1 and 2 contain the story of the Annunciation and an account of Jesus's childhood. Matthew Chapters 1:18-2:23 give different accounts of the infancy. I have put the stories from the two Gospels together to form a continuous narrative.

Matthew, Mark and Luke all make brief references to Mary's presence during Jesus's ministry, and John 2:1-11 recounts the story of the wedding feast at Cana. The dialogue with Mary at the Cross is taken from John 19:25-27.

Acts 1:14 records Mary's presence with Jesus's disciples and relations in Jerusalem. This mention of Mary comes between the stories of the Ascension and Pentecost. Christian tradition has usually maintained that Mary was present on both these occasions.

From at least the second century, Christians started telling stories about other events in Mary's life. The most important written account of these is contained in the *Protevangelium of James*[1] that records the story of Mary's conception and childhood. The detail about Anne and Joachim's meeting at the Golden Gate, which is often represented in art, comes from *The Gospel of Pseudo-Matthew*.[2]

---

[1] J. K. Elliott (ed.): *The Apocryphal New Testament*, Oxford: Clarendon Press, 1993, pp. 48–67. Extracts from these early stories are contained in J. K. Elliott (ed.): *The Apocryphal Jesus: Legends of the Early Church*, Oxford: Oxford University Press, 1996

[2] J. K. Elliott (ed.): *The Apocryphal New Testament*, p. 88

The stories of Mary's Assumption into Heaven are contained in writings that mostly come from a slightly later period. Their content varies from text to text, but the essential elements remain constant.[3]

Some of the material in *Mary's Story* is taken from art and folklore, for example, St. Anne teaching the Virgin to read was a popular motif in Medieval art and was revived in the nineteenth century. The goldfinch taking the thorn from Jesus's crown is also widespread in folklore. It is said to have acquired the red spot on its head when it drew out the thorn and was splashed with a drop of the Savior's blood. For this reason, the goldfinch is often shown in paintings and sculptures of the Virgin and Child.

Over the centuries, many people have had visions in which they have seen or been told about the life of the Virgin. Some of these visions have been quite authoritative, or have been generally held in high esteem. I used the accounts of Anne Catherine Emmerich's visions[4] for one or two details of *Mary's Story*. I also made use of the Abbé Orsini's *History of the Blessed Virgin Mary, Mother of God*, which gives a life of the Virgin made up from a variety of sources.[5]

[3]J. K. Elliott (ed.): *The Apocryphal New Testament*, pp. 691-723

[4]*The Life of the Blessed Virgin Mary from the Visions of Anne Catherine Emmerich* (tr. Michael Palairet): Tan Books, Rockford, Illinois, 1970

[5]Abbé Orsini: *The History of the Blessed Virgin Mary, Mother of God* (tr. F. C. Husenbeth): Virtue and Co., London, 1870